the world of little golden books™

Christmas is Golden

By Diane Muldrow

A GOLDEN BOOK · NEW YORK

CHRISTMAS IS a snowfall, fluffy and white.

From *Jingle Bells* by Kathleen N. Daly, illustrated by J. P. Miller, 1964.

Christmas is a fir tree, shimmering with light.

From *Christmas Carols,* arranged by Marjorie Wyckoff, illustrated by Corinne Malvern, 1946.

Christmas is a stocking, soft and red,

From *The Santa Claus Book* by Richard Scarry, 1965.

and the smell of warm, sweet gingerbread.

From *The Sweet Smell of Christmas* by Patricia Scarry, illustrated by J. P. Miller, 1970.

Christmas is quiet,

From *The Little Christmas Elf* by Nikki Shannon Smith, illustrated by Susan Mitchell, 2011.

and Christmas is noise—

From *Frosty the Snow Man,* retold by Annie North Bedford, illustrated by Corinne Malvern, 1950.

the laughter of pink-cheeked
girls and boys!

Christmas is wrapping a present
with care

From *The Poky Little Puppy's First Christmas* by Adelaide Holl, illustrated by Florence Sarah Winship, 1973.

and carols we sing in the cold, frosty air!

From *The Sweet Smell of Christmas* by Patricia Scarry,
illustrated by J. P. Miller, 1970.

From *The Animals' Christmas Eve* by Gale Wiersum, illustrated by Alex Steele Morgan, 2005.

It's the joy that came
on a midnight clear. . . .

Oh, Christmas is coming!

From *Christmas in the Country* by Barbara Collyer and John R. Foley, illustrated by Retta Worcester, 1950.

Christmas is near!

Christmas is
an ornament,
shiny and round,

From *Baby's Christmas* by Esther Wilkin, illustrated by Eloise Wilkin, 1959.

and Santa's black boots
not making a sound.

From *The Night Before Christmas* by Clement C. Moore, illustrated by Corinne Malvern, 1949.

It's the star in the sky
when angels did sing,

From *Christmas Carols*, arranged by Marjorie Wyckoff, illustrated by Corinne Malvern, 1946.

proclaiming the birth
of the newborn king!

It's cozy and warm,
whatever the weather,

From *Christmas in the Country* by Barbara Collyer and John R. Foley, illustrated by Retta Worcester, 1950.

this holiday about loved ones
being together.

From *Jingle Bells* by Kathleen N. Daly, illustrated by J. P. Miller, 1964.

Oh, Christmas is coming!

From *The Night Before Christmas* by Clement C. Moore, illustrated by Corinne Malvern, 1949.

Christmas is near!

From *The Golden Christmas Tree* by Jan Wahl, illustrated by Leonard Weisgard, 1988.

Christmas is golden . . .

CHRISTMAS IS HERE!

From *The Night Before Christmas* by Clement C. Moore, illustrated by Eloise Wilkin, 1955.